Jell-It Jack

ELLIE BEAUMONT

Illustrated by Frank Kennedy

The Story Characters

Nick Noble

Me

Liz, my sister

The Story Setting

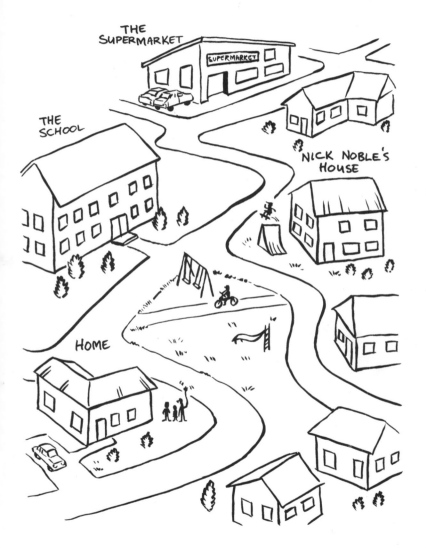

THE
SUPERMARKET

SUPERMARKET

THE
SCHOOL

NICK NOBLE'S
HOUSE

HOME

TABLE OF CONTENTS

Chapter 1
Ice Cream or Jell-It? . . 6

Chapter 2
Cherry. 8

Chapter 3
Free Jell-It 16

Chapter 4
The Wish . . . . 20

Chapter 5
Jell-It, Set, Go! . . . . . 24

Chapter 6
The Eat-Off . . . . 34

Chapter 7
What's Really Cool . . 40

Ice Cream or Jell-It?

Ice cream was out that summer. Jell-It gelatin was the thing. Jell-It with fruit, Jell-It in weird shapes, Jell-It any way you could get it.

There was going to be an Eat-Off tomorrow at Nick Noble's house. I could eat three bowls of Jell-It in 54 seconds. This would give me a chance to prove it.

CHAPTER 2

Cherry

The first stop was the supermarket.
I wanted cherry or lemon Jell-It. They
were the only flavors I liked.

There they were! A huge stack of Jell-It boxes. But can you believe it? They were all mango flavor!

Then I saw it. One box of cherry was in the bottom row. I had to have it!

I heard the rumble of wheels coming
toward me. I turned. It was Nick Noble
on his skateboard.

Quick! I thought. Grab the box of
cherry Jell-It.

Too late. Thump! Noble crashed into me, and I went flying into the stack. Jell-It boxes went everywhere!

Most of them landed on me.

I looked up to see Noble skating away.

Nick Noble was the most popular kid in our school. He had everything. He had the best skateboard, the coolest baseball cap, and now he had my cherry Jell-It, too.

CHAPTER 3

Free Jell-It

It looks like I'm stuck with mango, I thought, as I started to pick up the mess.

"Thanks," said the man from the store.
"I saw what happened. Here, have this
one for free."

He handed me a box of Jell-It. It was
an unusual color. It was called:

"Any Flavor You Wish For!"

Wow! Free Jell-It. Now that's cool.

CHAPTER 4

The Wish

My little sister Liz wanted to know what I was up to.

I told her about my run-in with Nick
Noble. I told her that we were having
an Eat-Off tomorrow afternoon.

"What's an Eat-Off?" asked Liz.

"It's a contest to see who can eat the most Jell-It in the shortest time," I said.

I got to work making the Jell-It. Then I made my wish.

"I wish for the coolest cherry Jell-It on the planet!"

CHAPTER 5

Jell-It, Set, Go!

"Is it ready? Is it ready?" asked Liz, as I took the Jell-It out of the fridge an hour later.

"It's still a bit wobbly," I said.
"Maybe we should move it into
smaller bowls."

"I know," said Liz. "I've got these
great shapes. We can make
stars and animals."

The wobbly Jell-It leaped out of the
bowl and onto the counter. A wobbling
Jell-It creature stood in front of us. His
face had a huge frown.

"No you don't!" he yelled. "I hate Jell-It molds. How would you like it if I turned you into a flower or a pig?"

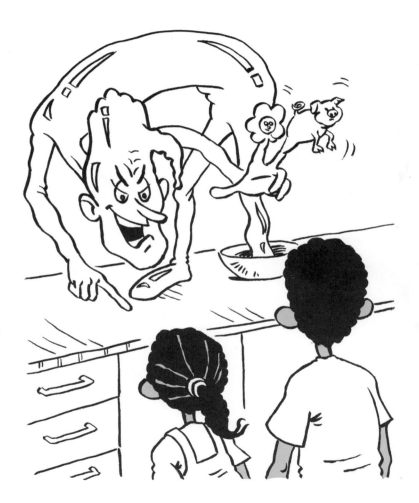

"Who, or what, are you?" I said. "All I wished for was cherry Jell-It."

"Not just cherry Jell-It! You wished for the coolest Jell-It on the planet. So now you've got it. Let's rock!"

He leaped from the counter, pressed
Play on our stereo, and began to
dance like you've never seen.

He wobbled, he grooved, and he twisted himself into a million shapes. He sucked himself into one end of a straw and out the other.

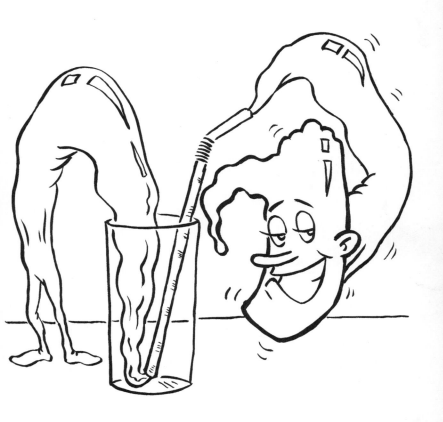

What could Liz and I do but dance along? He sure was the coolest Jell-It on the planet!

We called him Jell-It Jack.

The Eat-Off

"You should take him to the Eat-Off," said Liz. "When they see Jell-It Jack dance, you'll be the coolest kid in our school."

So the next day, we packed Jell-It Jack into my backpack.

"Phew!" said Jell-It Jack. "How long has this banana been in here?"

I couldn't wait to see Nick Noble's face when he saw Jell-It Jack.

It was a hot day and a long walk to school. Halfway there, I felt a wet dribble run down my back.

Oh no! Jell-It Jack was melting!

"Quick!" Liz yelled.

I poured Jell-It Jack into my lunch box. We ran home as fast as we could go.

By the time we got home, my lunch box was full of liquid. My heart sank.

I pushed my lunch box into the freezer. All we could do was wait.

CHAPTER 7

What's Really Cool

Half an hour later, I opened the freezer.
Then I opened my lunch box. The
Jell-It was still. Nothing moved.

"He's gone," whispered Liz.

"No I'm not. I'm freezing in here. And the frozen chicken is giving me some really weird looks."

Jell-It Jack pulled himself back into shape. He was a little smaller than before, but just as cool.

"It wasn't enough for you to have the coolest Jell-It in the world. You had to show me off to all of your friends, too."

I made up my mind then and there—
there are some things that are best to
keep to yourself.

GLOSSARY

flavor
the taste

frown
an unhappy face

liquid
like water

molds
forms used to
shape food

prove
to show something
is true

rumble
a low, rolling sound

stack
a big pile

wobbly
shaky

Ellie Beaumont

Ellie is different from the rest of us. She stays awake all night and sleeps during the day. When children go to school in the morning, she is just crawling into bed. She talks with owls, counts stars, and dreams of fantastic places. If you're ever restless in the night, Ellie suggests that you do what she does—start writing.

Frank Kennedy

Frank has been a cartoonist and illustrator for six years. But he has always had the urge to pick up a pencil and create pictures. His hobbies are writing, drawing, and reading.

sundance™

Copyright © 2001 Sundance/Newbridge, LLC

Published by Sundance Publishing
33 Boston Post Road West, Suite 440, Marlborough, MA 01752
800-343-8204

Copyright © text Ellie Beaumont
Copyright © illustrations Frank Kennedy

First published 1999 as Sparklers by
Blake Education, Locked Bag 2022, Glebe 2037, Australia
Exclusive United States Distribution: Sundance Publishing

ISBN 978-0-7608-8001-2

Printed by Nordica International Ltd.
Manufactured in Guangzhou, China
May, 2012
Nordica Job#: CA21200579
Sundance/Newbridge PO#: 226970